The Cubby

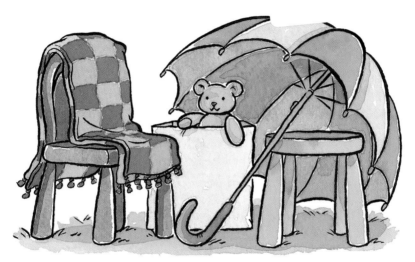

Monica Hughes
Illustrated by Julie Anderson

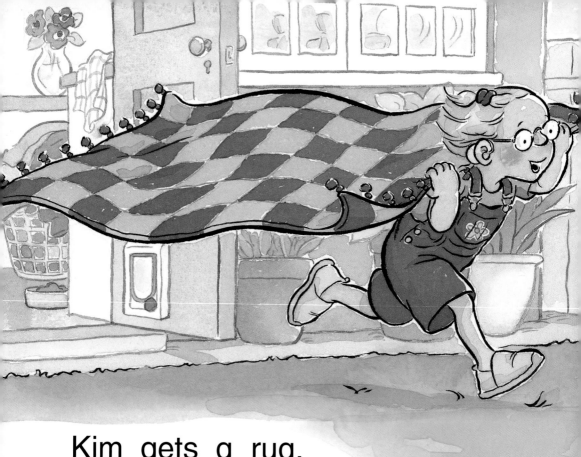

Kim gets a rug.

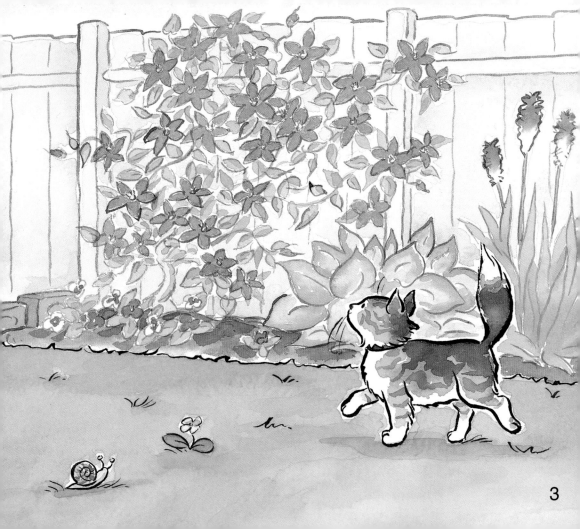

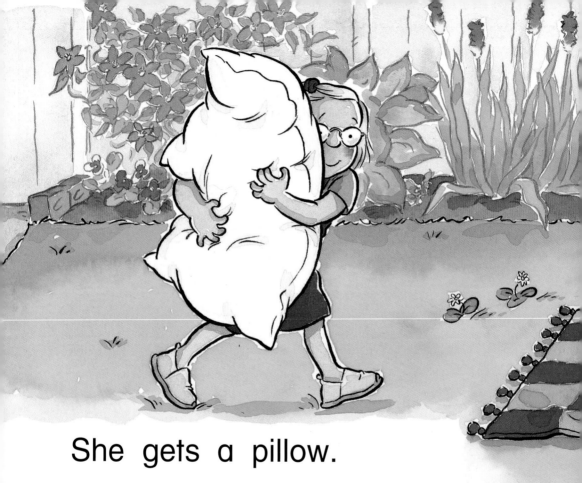

She gets a pillow.

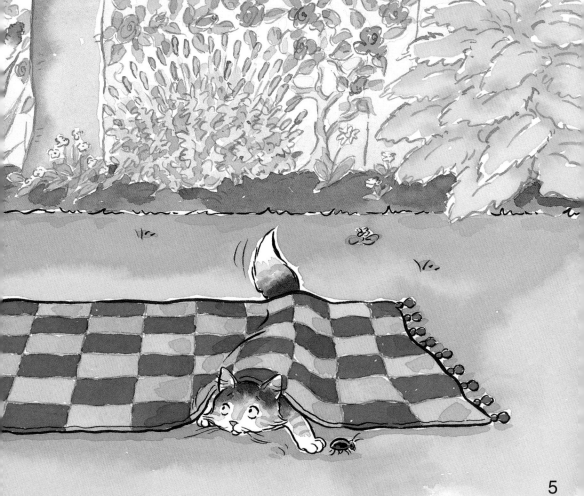

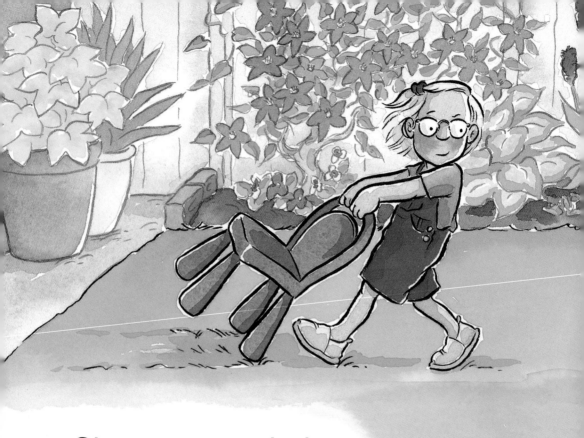

She gets a chair.

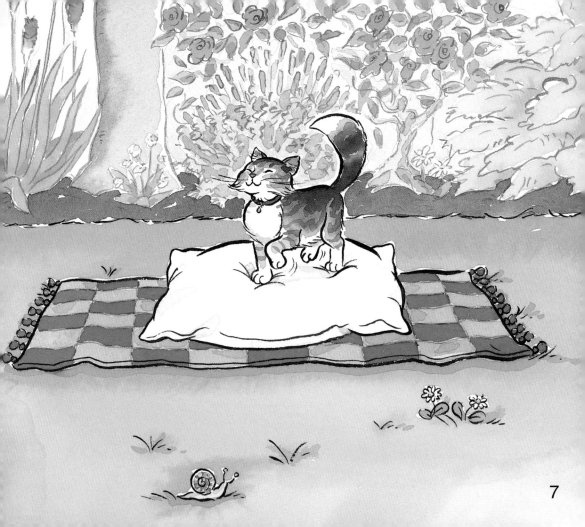

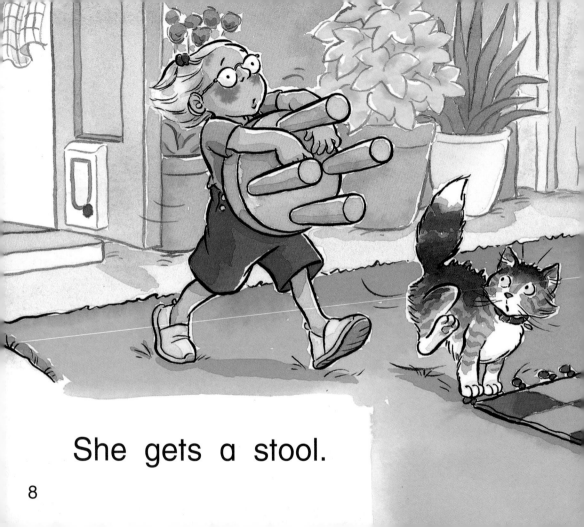

She gets a stool.

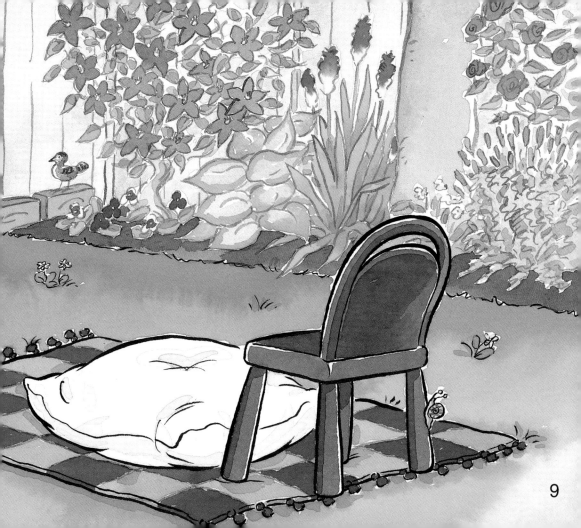

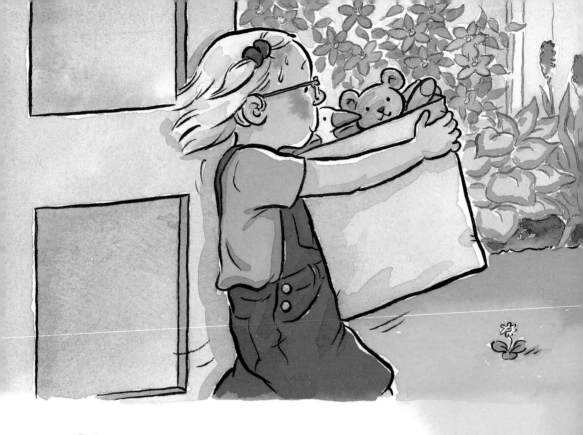

She gets a box.

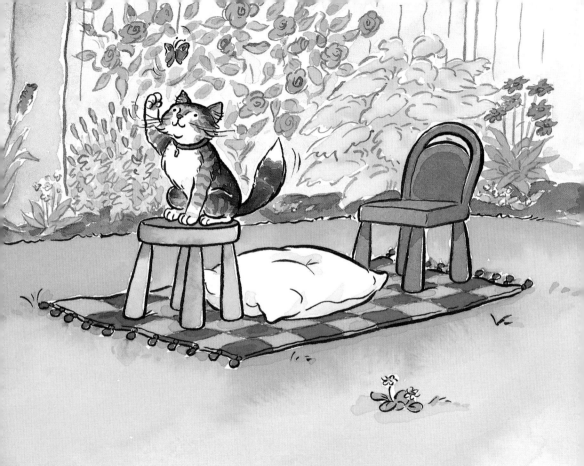

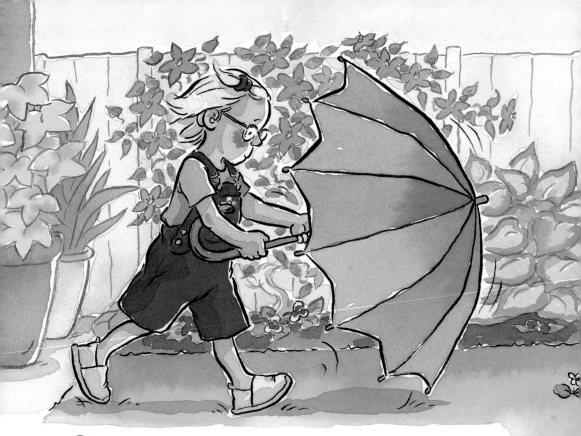

She gets an umbrella.

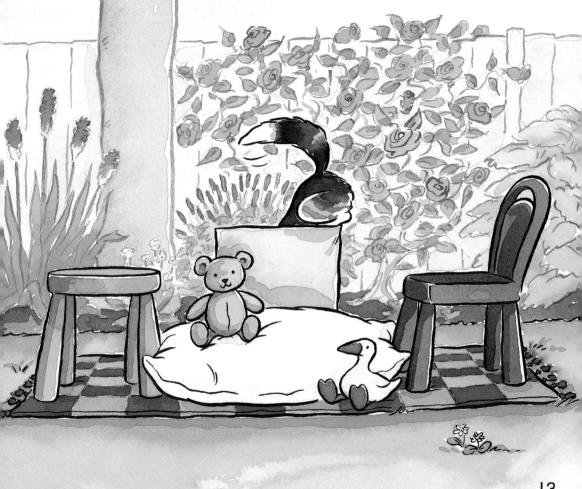

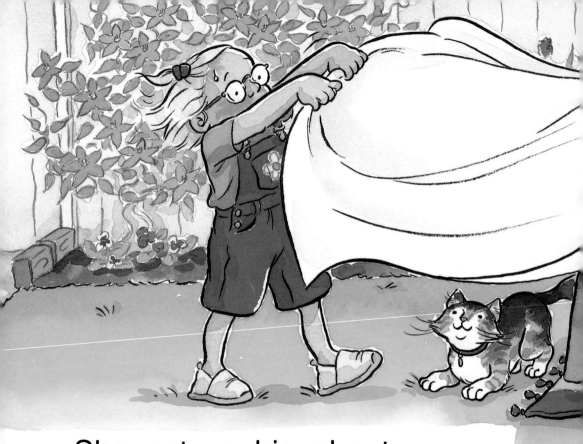

She gets a big sheet.

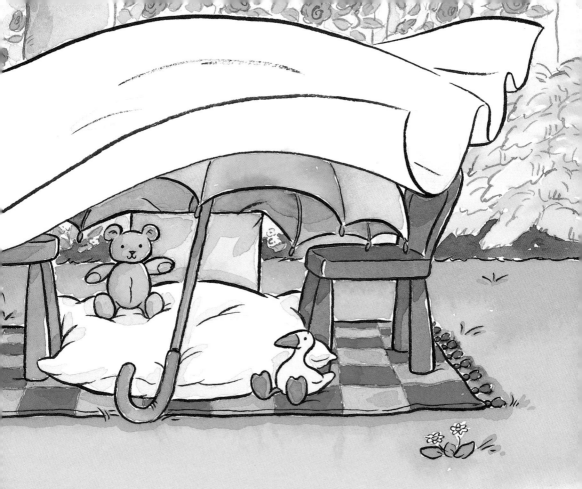

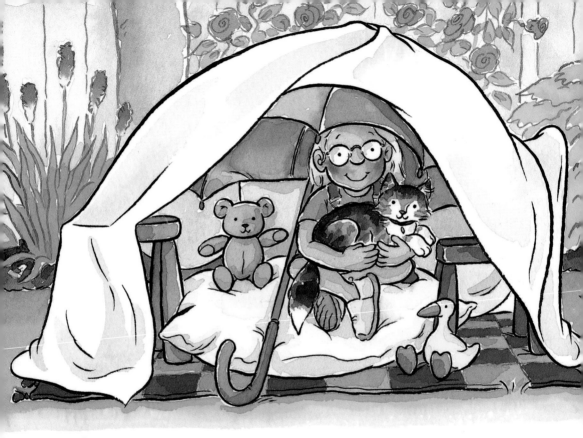

She gets in her cubbyhouse!